My Worst Friend

My Worst Friend

by P. J. Petersen

Illustrated by Meredith Johnson

SCHOLASTIC INC.

New York Toronto London Auckland Sydney
Mexico City New Delhi Hong Kong Buenos Aires

ISBN 0-439-74916-6

Text copyright © 1998 by P. J. Petersen.
Illustrations copyright © 1998 by Meredith Johnson. All rights reserved.
Published by Scholastic Inc., 557 Broadway, New York, NY 10012,
by arrangement with Dutton Children's Books, a member of Penguin Group (USA) Inc.
SCHOLASTIC and associated logos are trademarks
and/or registered trademarks of Scholastic Inc.

12 11 10 9 8 7 6 5 4 3 2   5 6 7 8 9 10/0

Printed in the U.S.A.   40

First Scholastic printing, April 2005

Designed by Alan Carr

For George and Sally Carpenter
—*P.J.P.*

For Avery, my best friend
—*M.J.*

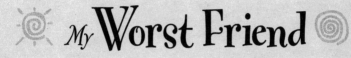

My Worst Friend

chapter 1

FRIDAY, OCTOBER 2

Sara Trent was up to something. She kept looking back at me with that nasty smile on her face. We were supposed to be drawing, but Sara had something else on her desk that she shoved under her paper whenever Mrs. Benson came around.

It was Friday afternoon art class. My worst subject. Today Mrs. Benson had brought in a limb from a maple tree. It had about ten leaves on it, different colors of red, gold, and brown. And we were supposed to use our colored pencils to draw it. Good luck.

What I had on my paper didn't even look like leaves. They could have been cat tracks or crooked stars. Mrs. Benson walked up and down the aisles saying, "That's wonderful," and "Oh, those look so real." When she got to mine, she said, "Keep working on it, Jennifer."

"This is dumb," I muttered. "If I want a picture of leaves, I'll get a camera."

Sam, who sat in front of me, held up his paper for me to see. "My picture was too boring, so I put in some extra stuff." His leaves were covered with bugs and caterpillars.

Sara got up from her desk and went to the pencil sharpener. When she stood up, a folded paper slipped to the floor. It was supposed to be an accident, but I knew better.

This was one of Sara's games. She'd write notes saying how much I liked some boy or how much I didn't like a teacher. Then she'd sign my name. She'd leave the note on the floor or in a book so somebody else would find it.

I headed up the aisle, scooping up the paper as I went. Sara finished sharpening her pencil, then smiled at me. "Your turn, Jenny." She always called me Jenny because she knew I hated it. A jenny, as Sara told everybody, is a female donkey, and she loved to get out the dictionary and show that.

"Thank you, Sara Louise," I said. She hated her middle name, so I used it all the time.

Back at my desk, I unfolded the note Sara had dropped. The message was printed in four colors:

Jenny Jones is so nosy that she sneaks around and picks up papers off the floor.

And, of course, Sara was watching me and laughing.

I took out a green pencil and wrote, "I blew my nose all over this paper." Then I folded the paper and took it to Sara's desk.

"You dropped this," I said.

Sara opened the note and laughed. She turned back and said, "I know that's not true, Jenny. You never wipe your nose anywhere but on your arm."

"Actually, today I wiped it on your coat," I told her. "The one hanging in the back. You can check it after school."

"That's enough, girls," Mrs. Benson said. She came and stood by my desk. I picked up a red pencil and started working on my crummy leaves again.

I think Sara was born rotten. She was probably one of those babies that always cry in the grocery store or at the movie theater. I don't know for sure. I didn't meet her until she was four. But she was plenty rotten by then.

I remember the first time I saw her. It was

my first day of preschool, and I was all excited. With my new red dress and new white tights, I looked great and I knew it. I came zipping in the front door and saw Sara. "Hi there," I shouted.

Sara was wearing jeans and a Mickey Mouse T-shirt. She walked over to me and said, "You look dumb."

I couldn't believe it. I almost started to cry. But I stuck out my tongue instead.

And, of course, the teacher saw me. "That's not the way we do things here," she said. So I had been at preschool for fifteen seconds, and I was already in trouble. And it was Sara's fault.

That same day Sara asked me to play with her in the sandbox. Right away she started putting sand inside my white tights. "You'll like this," she said. "It feels good. It cools you off."

I didn't think the sand felt good at all. But I didn't say so. I didn't want to hurt Sara's feelings. And, of course, my tights were ruined.

The next day Mom had me wear jeans to preschool. So Sara got what she wanted. I was too dumb to know that, though. I hadn't been around sneaky kids before.

And Sara was as sneaky as they came. At juice time she kept looking up at the ceiling. "See the spider?" she whispered. And I'd look up. But I couldn't see a spider. And every time I looked up, she grabbed my juice and drank some. I didn't catch on for a long time.

One day at preschool we found a worm on the grass. Sara grabbed it and held it up. "This is my favorite kind of worm. It's really yummy."

"You eat worms?"

"Sure," she said. "They're great. They're like chocolate. Only better." She moved away from me. "I saw this one first. I get to eat it."

"You can have it," I told her.

"Goody. I love worms." She started to put it in her mouth, then stopped. "You're my friend. I could share."

"No way," I said.

Sara saw she couldn't trick me into eating a worm, so she tried something else.

"You eat worms all the time," she said.

"I do not."

"You know the chocolate-chip cookies we get here? They're made out of worms."

"They are not," I said.

"Yes, they are," Sara said. "They're made out of yummy worms just like this one." And she opened her mouth, popped in the worm, and ate it.

Looking back now, I don't think she actually ate that worm. She might have, though. She'd do just about anything for a trick.

That morning I was sure the worm went into her mouth. And she got exactly what she wanted. For a long time after that, I let her have all my chocolate-chip cookies.

In kindergarten she spilled apple juice on me, then made everybody think I wet my pants. She didn't lie about it. She was too smart for that. She just kept pointing at my pants and saying, "She didn't wet her pants. That's apple juice." So, of course, nobody believed it was apple juice.

In the years since then, she hadn't changed much. She was still nasty and sneaky. But she was smart about it. If you were her friend, she could be really nice. She remembered your dog's name and noticed when your hair was different and brought you little surprises.

But if you *weren't* her friend, she could be really rotten. She'd get you on your bad-hair days, and she'd remember every dumb thing you ever did.

So most people stayed friends with her. Except me, of course. She was always rotten to me. Her latest thing was telling creepy boys that I liked them. She was really good at making the boys think they had tricked her into telling them the secret. And she always picked somebody like Robby Dodge, this boy who burps "The Star-Spangled Banner."

I learned to fight back. I had to. And nothing made her happier. She loved to get me in a battle—saying nasty things back and forth—because she could usually outlast me.

So I had to find other ways to beat her.

Sara wanted to be the best at everything. And even being the best wasn't good enough. If she got the highest grade on a test, she'd say she didn't even study. When her essay on "What Christmas Means to Me" won the newspaper contest, she said, "It's okay, I guess. I wrote it in about fifteen minutes."

So it was fun to see her when she wasn't the best. She'd get red in the face and give me dirty looks. I'd smile and say, "Maybe you'll do better next time." That really made her squirm.

She almost turned purple when my volcano project won the grand prize in the science fair. She told everybody that my father did all the work. But I just smiled and said to her, "Don't feel too bad. You got second place."

My mother liked Sara's mother. So our mothers tried to make us be friends. But it never worked.

I told Mom how rotten Sara was, but Mom just said, "I know she's difficult sometimes. But you're going to be around difficult people all your life. You can get along."

Difficult. That was one way to put it.

Mom didn't say so, but I always thought Sara's mother was difficult, too. If somebody didn't agree with her, she would start talking faster and faster, and her voice would get higher and higher. But Mom said she was interesting.

About once a month our mothers would set things up, and Sara and I had to play together. When we were little, we sat around and watched television. That way, we didn't have to talk. But when we got older, we played games like checkers or basketball. Games where we could try to beat each other.

"I'm going to smash you," Sara would say.

"I'm going to destroy you so bad, they won't be able to find the pieces."

"I wish you wouldn't get so excited," I'd say. "You always feel so bad when you lose."

These weren't games. These were wars.

"You and Sara seem to be getting along better now," Mom said one time after we took Sara home. "I knew you two could be friends if you worked at it."

I told Sara about that, and we both cracked up laughing. But then Sara said, "Your mom's right, in a way. I like everybody in the world. Even you."

"Oh, sure."

"I just like you less than anybody else. You're my worst friend."

I laughed. "And you're *my* worst friend. You come below Robby Dodge and that snooty Valerie that moved away last year. And Freddy What's-his-name from *Nightmare on Elm Street*. And that boxer that bit off the guy's ear."

"Think of all the liars and whiners and brag-

gers and tattletales that we don't even know," Sara said. "They're all ahead of you."

"Worst friends," I said. "Worst friends forever." We laughed and gave each other a high five. Then we crossed our eyes and stuck out our tongues.

chapter 2

FRIDAY, OCTOBER 9

It was the Friday before Columbus Day, the day of our big debate. That week our class had been talking about Christopher Columbus. I had said he hadn't really discovered America, so of course Sara said he had.

"He didn't know where he was," I said.

"But he found America all the same," Sara said.

"It was just luck," I went on. "He thought he was in Asia."

"So what?" Sara said. "If you're lucky and find a dollar, you still have the dollar."

We were just getting warmed up, but our teacher, Ms. Diaz, stopped us. She said we should have a debate on the subject. She checked her calendar and decided that the debate should be on the Friday before Columbus Day.

Sara and I each had three people on our side. I had Brenda, Nai, and Eddie. Brenda and Nai had their speeches ready. Eddie didn't want to make a speech. "I'll just make faces when Sara talks," he said.

The four of us met at noon to practice. Sara came over to us. She had a big bunch of girls with her. "You're dead meat," she told us, and the girls with her laughed. "Wait till you see our secret weapon."

"Yeah," Vicky Waite said. She was always one of Sara's bunch.

"We have a secret weapon, too," I told them. "We're right."

"You're dreaming, Squirrel Cheeks," Sara said, and Vicky laughed out loud.

"Do you think she has a secret weapon?" Brenda asked after they left.

"Yes," I said. "But we'll beat her anyway."

When we came in from lunch, Ms. Diaz was correcting tests at her desk. She always wore bright colors, but today's red, white, and blue dress was *really* bright. She called it her flag dress.

She wrote on the tests with purple and green ink. And she used rubber stamps that said GENIUS and WOW! Eddie stopped at her desk and begged her to stamp his hand. Most teachers wouldn't do something like that. But Ms. Diaz stamped GENIUS on his arm six times and said, "I'll be expecting genius work from you this afternoon."

"Ms. Diaz," I said.

She turned to me and raised her stamp. "You

want me to do your arm, too?" She laughed when I jerked back my hand.

Just then Sara and Vicky came in the door, carrying cardboard boxes. "Hey, loser," Sara said to me, "you know what's in the boxes? Our secret weapon."

"One good thing about having only two teams," I said. "At least you can get second place."

Sara smiled. "I see you got a new dress for the debate," she said. "What Dumpster did it come from?"

"Isn't it a little early for a Halloween mask?" I said. "Oh, that's your face." I had been saving that one for a while, but it seemed like a good time for it.

Sara laughed out loud. "That's a good one, Jenny. Is that what your mother said to you this morning?"

I went down the aisle to my desk. Sara would keep going that way forever. Nothing could make her happier than a good fight.

Except having me fall on my face in a mud puddle.

Sara and Vicky opened their boxes, and Sara called out, "For Columbus Day, which is named for the man who discovered America, we made cookies." Everybody clapped. Even the people on my team.

"Why are you clapping?" I asked Eddie. "The cookies are their secret weapon."

"Give me a break, Jones," Eddie said. "I'll always clap for cookies."

Sara wanted to pass out cookies right away. But Ms. Diaz told her to wait until after the debate. Sara held up a cookie and said, "See? They're shaped like ships, the three ships that Columbus sailed in when he discovered America."

We had our debate. I don't want to brag, but my team made Sara's bunch look sick. Nai got out the dictionary. "I am still learning English," he said. "So I have to look up many words. *Discover* means to be the first to find something. But when Mr. Columbus came to the islands, people were already living there. So he wasn't the first."

Sara's team should have given up right then. They didn't, of course. Sara went on and on. She mentioned the ships and the cookies about twenty times.

When Ms. Diaz finally stopped us, Sara wanted the class to vote. "Let's vote," she said. "Then we'll celebrate with the cookies."

But Ms. Diaz said there was no reason to vote. "I think you're all winners."

"She didn't want you to get your feelings hurt, Goat Breath," Sara said to me.

Sara and Vicky passed out the cookies. Big sugar cookies with the names of the ships written in red frosting. "I want the *Santa Maria*," Eddie said. "It has more frosting."

When Sara got to my desk, she handed me a cookie and whispered, "I made this one special just for you. I spit on it."

She thought she had me. If I gave away my

cookie, she'd laugh at me for believing her. If I ate it, she'd still laugh.

But I spoiled her fun by trading my cookie to Eddie for a Tootsie Roll. When you've been around Sara as long as I have, you learn to be sneaky.

chapter 3

TUESDAY, OCTOBER 20

It was Tuesday. That meant physical education with Mr. Craig and pizza for lunch in the cafeteria. And Sara was absent for the second day in a row. Things were looking good.

My friend Brenda was talking about her big sister, Mary. All the girls in Mrs. Wilson's sixth-grade class had a doll to take care of for a week. They were supposed to treat the doll like it was a real baby and keep it with them all the time.

"My sister's going to be a terrible mother," Brenda said. "She dropped her baby on the floor this morning, and our dog tried to eat it."

"You know what Jackie Martin did?" Eddie said. "She forgot and left her doll in the band room all weekend."

"The whole thing is stupid," Brenda said. "Last Wednesday, when they got the dolls, all those girls were lovey and sweet. Now they're sick of carrying them around. Mary says the whole thing is a big pain."

"That's why Mrs. Wilson does it," I said. "She wants them to see that it's not easy to take care of a baby."

Nai laughed. "I could tell them that. They should use my little brother. He waits until my whole family is asleep. Then he cries and cries."

"Mrs. Wilson ought to make the boys do it, too," Brenda said. "Can't you see old Alan

Benson carrying a doll?" Alan was the meanest boy in the sixth grade. His idea of fun was dumping some little kid into a garbage can, headfirst.

"The boys get it easy," Brenda went on. "They just have to find out how much it costs to drive a car and figure out how much they'd spend driving around for a week."

"I'd rather have a car than a baby," another girl said.

"Me, too," Nai said, laughing. "You know anybody with a nice car who wants to trade? They can have my brother."

Sam came running into the room just before the last bell rang. He had his arms wrapped around his stomach. So I knew he had something hidden inside his shirt.

Sam's desk is right in front of mine. When he slid into his chair, I asked him, "What's in your shirt?"

Sam started to laugh. "This is so neat. Don't tell anybody."

"What is it?"

"You know the girls in Mrs. Wilson's class? They have those dolls they're supposed to treat like babies."

"What about it?"

Sam reached inside his shirt. A doll's head poked out between two buttons. Sam shoved the doll back. "Don't tell."

"That's kidnapping," I said. "Whose is it?"

"Gloria's. Isn't that neat?"

Gloria was a bossy sixth-grader. If somebody had to have her baby stolen, I'd pick Gloria.

"You'll get in trouble," I told Sam.

"It serves Gloria right," Sam said. "She went and played tetherball. Left her baby lying on the ground. I felt sorry for the poor little thing." Sam leaned across the aisle. "Hey, Brenda, look what I got."

Brenda broke out laughing. "Is it my sister's?"

"It's Gloria's," Sam said, "but I'm adopting it."

The last bell rang. Jacob Smalley came running into the room. "I'm not late," he called out. He lived right across the street from the school, but he was always the last one to get to class.

"Close the door, Jake," Ms. Diaz said. She got up from her desk and came down the aisle. That day she was wearing a red dress with big white stars. She stood by Sam's desk and held out her hand.

"What's the matter?" Sam asked.

Ms. Diaz didn't even look at him. She just kept her hand out.

Sam took the doll out of his shirt. "I found it on the playground," he said, handing it to Ms. Diaz.

Ms. Diaz nodded. "I really didn't think you brought it from home." She walked back and set the doll on the file cabinet.

"Too bad, Sam," Eddie said. "She took away your dolly."

Robby Dodge burped out the first part

of "Rock-a-bye, Baby." One or two boys laughed.

Mrs. Diaz sat on her desk and looked at us. "I have some bad news," she said. "Sara is very sick."

Half the class turned to look at me. I tried not to smile. But maybe a little smile slipped onto my face.

"We're going to make cards for her," Ms. Diaz said. "We want her to know that we're all thinking about her."

"We're all thinking she should stay sick," I whispered.

Sam laughed and looked back at me. "That's mean."

"I'm just telling the truth," I said. "If I wanted to be mean, I could do lots worse."

Ms. Diaz passed out some special paper to use for cards. A month before that, the class had made cards for me. I had sprained my ankle playing soccer. It had been neat to get cards from everybody. Except Sara.

Sara had drawn a nice picture on the outside of the card. But on the inside, this is what she wrote:

> *Roses are red.*
> *Violets are blue.*
> *You hurt your footsie.*
> *Boo Hoo Hoo.*

I folded my paper to make a card. Then I sat and looked at it. I didn't know what to write. Right away I thought of something rotten:

> *Mickey's a mouse.*
> *Bambi's a deer.*
> *I hope you don't come back*
> *Until next year.*

But I wouldn't send something like that. I might think about it. But I wouldn't do it.

In front of me, Sam was scribbling away. He

was giggling the whole time. "What are you writing?" I whispered.

Sam held up his card so that I could read it over his shoulder:

> *Dear Sara,*
> *I hope you hurry back.*
> *I really miss you.*
> *Do you miss me?*
> *I can't wait to see you again.*

I couldn't believe it. "You're writing that to Sara?"

Sam kept laughing. "Yeah, but I'm signing Clint's name. He's absent today."

Somebody called out, "Does this have to be a poem?"

"It can be a poem or a little note—whatever you want," Ms. Diaz said. Then she looked right at me. "Just so it's nice." I started to say something, but she winked at me.

It was hard to write that card. I didn't want

to say anything mean. But if I was nice to Sara, she'd think I was being a fake. I ended up writing, "Get well soon. School isn't the same without you." I liked that note. You could take it two ways. And Sara would know that.

chapter 4

THURSDAY, OCTOBER 22

I first heard the news on Thursday during third period—English and reading with Mr. Craig. At eleven o'clock every morning, he came to our room, and Ms. Diaz taught math and science to his class. Some of the girls in our class could hardly wait for third period. They were always talking about how cute Mr. Craig was. When he got a haircut or wore a new shirt, they went crazy.

Mr. Craig came rushing into class just after the last bell rang. "We've got work to do," he shouted. That evening was Back-to-School Night, and most people hadn't finished their reading projects.

Pretty soon people were fighting over staplers and tape. Somebody had spilled glue on the floor and just left it there. Mr. Craig couldn't find the glue spiller, so he said the first person he saw loafing would clean up the glue. That made everybody act busy.

We were doing projects about our library books. We couldn't just do book reports. We had to do something fancy. Some people did posters. Some made book covers. Some were cutting pictures out of magazines and pasting them onto poster paper. That's called a collage, but it looks like a mess.

Two girls had read *Night of the Twisters*, a book about tornados. They had built a scene inside a cardboard box, with torn-up houses and turned-over toy cars. Sam told them they should take apart some old dolls and leave arms and legs lying around.

My project was finished—a cover and pictures for my book. So Mr. Craig had me helping other people. I helped Nai glue fish onto his *Island of the Blue Dolphins* poster. Then I cut some pictures out of a hunting magazine for Eddie's collage. Eddie hadn't read his book, *The Yearling*, so he didn't care what kind of pictures he used.

Ms. Diaz already had our science reports up on the wall. After helping Eddie, I went over and looked at them. I could spot Sara's report right away. She had done it on her mother's computer. The report had fancy lettering and graphs in five colors. She even had a blue border around each page.

Brenda came and stood by me. "Look at that," I told her. "It makes mine look sick."

Brenda didn't even look up. "You know what Julie said? She said Sara's having an operation. She might die."

"Oh, sure," I said.

"She heard Ms. Diaz talking to some other teachers."

"They were probably talking about some TV show. If Sara was having an operation, Ms. Diaz would have told us."

"Just what I need," Mr. Craig called out. "Two girls with nothing to do." He handed me a roll of paper towels. "It's glue time."

"That's not fair," I said. "I already—" But Mr. Craig just gave me that dumb smile he has. So Brenda and I cleaned up the glue.

Jacob laughed at us and whispered, "Keep scrubbing, girls."

"You spilled it, didn't you?" Brenda asked.

He giggled. "I'll never tell."

"You wait," I told him. "We're gonna put glue on your chair. Not right now. Later on. When you're not expecting it. You'll end up stuck to your chair." We didn't do it, but for that whole week, Jacob checked his chair every time he sat down.

Mr. Craig started setting up projects on the back counter. "Come on," he yelled. "It's almost noon. Even if you're not done, bring what you have."

We spent the rest of the period trying to fit everything onto the counter. Some people wanted their projects right in front. Others tried to hide theirs. And somebody had spilled glue again, and everybody stepped in it. So we spent the first part of lunch hour cleaning the floor.

While we scrubbed, Mr. Craig moved the projects around. The whole counter looked like something from *Night of the Twisters*. But every time he moved a project, somebody complained: "You can't even see mine." "Why does his go in front? Mine's just as good."

When Mr. Craig finally quit, the counter looked messy, but not quite so bad. I knew things wouldn't stay where they were. And I was right. People moved projects all afternoon.

———

All during lunch, I kept thinking about Sara. I didn't really believe what I'd heard, but I wanted to be sure. When I came back to the room, I stopped and said to Ms. Diaz, "There's a stupid rumor going around about Sara. She's not in the hospital, is she?"

I expected Ms. Diaz to laugh, but she gave me a funny look instead. "I'm supposed to hear some news about Sara anytime now. When it comes in, I'll let you know."

The last thing I wanted to do was wait. I moved up close to Ms. Diaz and whispered, "She really *is* in the hospital, isn't she?"

Ms. Diaz motioned me close, then whispered in my ear, "When I get some news, I'll give it to you."

"Come on," I said. "Please."

Ms. Diaz shook her head and waved me away. So I figured Sara was in the hospital. And I knew Ms. Diaz wasn't going to tell me anything until she was good and ready.

That was the longest afternoon of the year.

Ms. Diaz rushed around, stapling papers on the wall and shoving junk into the file cabinets. We were supposed to write welcome letters to our parents, then clean out our desks.

Nai raised his hand and asked, "Can I come tonight?"

"Back-to-School Night is supposed to be for parents only," Ms. Diaz told him.

"But I have to be here to read my note to my mom and dad. They can't read English yet."

"Then you get a special invitation," Ms. Diaz said. She took out a piece of paper and wrote PLEASE COME TO BACK-TO-SCHOOL NIGHT in purple ink. She used a rubber stamp to put stars all over it, then gave it to Nai. "We'll be happy to have you."

Sam found an old bologna sandwich in his desk. It was covered with black fuzz. "You hungry?" he asked me, shoving the nasty thing in my face. Then he ran around the room, showing it to everybody.

"We'll put it on the wall," Ms. Diaz said.

"Sam's art project." She actually stapled it up there, but she took it down later.

We were supposed to read our library books when we finished our letters. But I couldn't keep my mind on my book. I kept looking over at Sara's empty desk. I knew something was really wrong. Otherwise, Ms. Diaz would have told me what was happening.

"This is dumb," Eddie said. He sat right behind me. "Why should I write a welcome letter? My dad's not coming. He works nights."

"Then my dad can sit in your desk," I said. "My mom and dad will both be here."

"What's your dad's name?" Eddie asked. "I'll write him a letter."

"It's Harold," I said. "But you might want to call him Mr. Jones."

"Harold's fine."

Eddie scribbled away for a long time. "How do you spell *daughter*?" he asked me.

I told him, then asked, "What are you saying?"

Eddie laughed. "None of your business. You're not supposed to read other people's mail."

But when he finished, he couldn't wait to show me the note:

Dear Harold,

How are you? I am fine. Welcome to our class. See all the writing on this desk? I did NOT do any of it. Honest.

Your daughter is nice most of the time. But she won't let me copy her homework. Tell her to help out her pals.

Your friend,
Eddie

"He'll like that," I told Eddie.

Eddie smiled. "You better be nice to me. I might tell him how you were smoking out behind the backstop."

"That's a lie. I wouldn't smoke if you paid me. That was some dumb sixth-grader."

"Yeah, but your dad doesn't know that."

Five minutes before the final bell, I went up and asked Ms. Diaz, "Aren't you going to tell us about Sara? You said you would."

Ms. Diaz looked at the clock and let out a sigh. "I didn't realize it was so late." She got everybody to sit down. Then she leaned against her desk and took a long breath. "I have some news about Sara," she said slowly.

I wanted to scream for her to hurry up.

"Sara is in the hospital. She's having an operation today. I was hoping we'd hear by now. But I'm sure everything will be fine."

"What's the matter with her?" Brenda asked.

"What kind of operation?" I called out.

"One of the sixth-graders says it's a brain tumor," Jacob said. "He oughta know. He lives right across the street from Sara."

Half the class let out sounds like "Oooh" and "Oh no." Vicky, who had the desk behind Sara's, screamed and started to sob.

Ms. Diaz held up her hand. "There's a little growth. That's all a tumor is. The doctors are

going to remove it, and Sara will be fine. I didn't want everybody worrying about it."

"I think you should have told us," I said. My voice got louder than I meant it to.

"Maybe," Ms. Diaz said. "But I was hoping I could wait and tell you when it was all over. In a few days I'll take her a balloon bouquet. I'll get a card, and we can all sign it."

"Maybe that's why Sara was so smart," Sam said. "She had all that extra stuff in there."

"That's not funny," I shouted. "She has a brain tumor."

"Calm down," Ms. Diaz said. "Sara is getting excellent care. I expect her back here in class in a week or two."

We all sat there waiting for the bell. The only sound in the room was Vicky sobbing. I felt like joining her. But I also felt like hitting something. Or somebody.

While Mom and Dad went to Back-to-School Night, I stayed with Mrs. Black, our next-door neighbor. She had worked as a nurse when she was younger. I asked her about brain tumors.

"You don't have one," she said.

"I didn't say I did."

Mrs. Black shook her head. "These days people get a headache and they think it's a brain tumor."

I told her somebody on a TV show had one. So she told me all about tumors—people who had died and ones who had lost their memories.

When Mrs. Black saw me getting worried, she started asking questions. I told her about Sara. After that, all of Mrs. Black's stories were about people who got well.

But I was still worried.

When Mom and Dad came back, I ran out to meet them. Dad started in about Eddie's note. I looked at Mom, and she said, "Sara's fine." But Mom's voice didn't sound right.

"Is she coming back to school pretty soon?" I asked.

"Not right away. She'll have to stay in the hospital for a while. She'll be having some treatments."

Mrs. Black had told me about treatments—before she heard about Sara. "Are they going to give her drugs that make her hair fall out?" I asked.

"Maybe," Mom said. "But she's going to be fine."

Mom's no good at hiding things. She was worried. So I was worried, too. But I didn't want to say anything out loud. I turned to Dad. "Did you see my book project?"

chapter 5

TUESDAY, NOVEMBER 24

Two days before Thanksgiving, Mom drove me to the hospital after school. We were going to visit Sara. I was carrying a shopping bag full of letters the class had written that day. I also had a card from Mr. Craig's class and a GET WELL SOON banner the sixth-graders had made on the computer.

Up until then Sara had been too sick for

many visitors. Ms. Diaz had been to the hospital twice. And Mrs. Benson, our art teacher, had taken a quilt that our class had made. (We each did a square of the quilt. Then Mrs. Benson sewed all the squares together.)

On Monday Sara's mother had called Mom and said that Sara might like some company. "This wasn't Sara's idea," I told Mom. "Sara can't stand to be in the same room with me."

"Oh, I think she'll be glad to see you," Mom said.

But I knew better. So did everybody in my class. Nobody could believe I was the one going to the hospital. "It's just not fair," Vicky said. "I should go, not Jennifer."

"I didn't ask for this," I told her. "I wish you could go in my place." But that just made her madder.

I was kind of scared on the way to the hospital. I didn't know what to expect. I knew that Sara was sick, but in some funny way, it didn't seem real.

I didn't know what I could say to her. Sara and I never talked like regular people. And I couldn't walk into a hospital room and say, "Hi, Buzzard Breath," the way I usually did.

I could give her the letters and the banner. And I could tell her what we'd been studying in school. Then what?

"We won't stay long," Mom said when we got out of the car. "Sara's still pretty weak from her treatments."

"That's fine," I said.

"And she probably won't be at her best," Mom went on. "She's been through a lot."

"This is a bad idea," I said. "They should have had somebody else come."

I started feeling sick the minute we walked through the front door of the hospital. People in uniforms were rushing around, and all the visitors looked worried. An old man in a wheel-chair was staring at the wall and mumbling.

Sara was in Room 231, which was on the second floor. Mom and I took an elevator, then walked down some creepy hallways. The air smelled like medicine, and the sound of our footsteps echoed off the walls.

Mom put her hand on my shoulder. "Don't look so sad. You'll scare poor Sara."

I smiled—for half a second. I decided that I would just say hi and ask Sara how she was feeling. Maybe she'd do a lot of talking. She usually did.

The door to Room 231 was open. I looked in and saw Sara sitting up in bed. Except that she didn't look like Sara. Her face had no color at all, and her lips were kind of blue.

But I didn't really see her face. Not at first. I saw the top of her head. Her hair was gone.

She looked like an old, old lady. Or with her hair gone—an old, old man. Seeing her with that sick-white face and round head, you couldn't believe she'd ever played tetherball or done a cartwheel.

I couldn't believe it. I knew Sara was sick, but I was picturing the same old Sara—maybe

with a headache. I wasn't ready for this white-faced ghost.

I stepped back and turned to Mom. I couldn't go into the room yet. I was afraid I'd start crying or throw up.

"Look what the cat dragged in," Sara called out. Her voice was a little shaky, but she sounded like her old self.

Mom pushed me ahead of her into the room. "Hello, Sara," Mom said.

Up close, Sara looked even worse—skinny, with purple circles around her eyes. I pulled back the corners of my mouth and hoped it looked like a smile. I couldn't say anything yet.

"Hi." Sara grabbed a San Francisco Giants baseball cap and put it on with the bill facing sideways. "You caught me with my cap off."

"Hi," I managed to say. I tried to keep my eyes on her eyes so that I wouldn't look up at her hair—or where her hair used to be.

But Sara caught on right away. She reached up and lifted off her cap. "What do you think,

Bacteria Brain? Pretty cute, huh?" She turned away from me so that I could see the big pink scar on the back of her head. I looked down at her pillow. I was afraid I was going to be sick.

Right then I just felt sorry for Sara. I forgot every bad thing she'd ever done to me. I wanted to say something to her, something that would make her feel better. But I couldn't think of a thing.

"It'll grow back soon," Mom said. "A woman I know had the same thing. She said her hair was easier to work with afterward."

Sara rubbed her bare head with her hand. "We'll see. It's sure easy to work with right now." She looked at me. "Hey, Mouse Meat, you want to feel it?"

I stepped back without meaning to. "That's okay."

"Don't get scared," Sara said. "You won't catch a tumor by touching me."

So I put my left hand on her head, being

careful to stay away from the scar. "Hmmm," I muttered. I didn't know what else to say.

Mom felt Sara's head and said, "It's like a baby's."

Sara looked me straight in the eye, that little show-me-something smile on her face. "They made you come and see me, huh?"

How was I supposed to answer that? "I brought you some stuff," I said, looking down at the shopping bag. "Letters and a card. And the sixth-graders made a banner and everybody signed it."

Sara snorted. "A banner? Big whoop. One of those tacky two-minute computer jobs, right? What am I supposed to do with it?"

I looked around her room. The one blank wall was covered with the quilt and cards. Even the TV set, which was hanging from the ceiling, had cards taped to the sides.

"You seem to be out of room," Mom said.

"There's room in the wastebasket," Sara said. "Good place for it."

"Oh, Sara," Mom said, laughing. But I knew Sara wasn't joking.

"You can leave the bag here by the stand," Sara said. "Mom and I can look at the stuff later."

I set down the bag. "You want us to unroll the banner?" I asked.

Sara shook her head. "I know what it says. Get well soon, right?" She snorted and waved me away.

Mom and I stood and looked at her for a long time. Finally Mom asked, "Is there anything you'd like, Sara? I'll be happy to go down to the gift shop for you."

"Maybe some new hair," Sara said.

"What color?" Mom asked. "Red, green?"

Sara smiled for the first time. "I could use some Breath Savers," she said. "I just ran out. My mouth is really dry all the time."

"I'll go get 'em," I said.

But Mom was already heading for the door. "I'll go. You girls go ahead and talk."

Once Mom was gone, Sara turned and looked out the window. I stood by the bed and tried to think of something to say. I felt really stupid. I felt sorry for Sara and wanted to help her. But I was standing there like a dope. And I was afraid I might throw up any minute.

I decided that I had to say something, even if it was dumb. "Everybody said to say hi," I began, forcing back the corners of my mouth. "We're all really sorry you got sick. I know it's been hard for—"

Sara held up her hand. "Come on, Jenny. That's enough of that nicey-nice junk. You'll make me puke."

"It's true," I said. "Everybody's worried about you. When we first heard about your operation, Vicky Waite broke out crying."

Sara groaned. "Vicky starts bawling when she gets a hangnail. And what about you, Roadkill? Did you cry big tears?"

I kept the smile on my face. "They say you're going home soon."

"Not soon enough," Sara said. "The food's horrible here. Worse than the barfy school cafeteria. And I never get any sleep. All night long people are yelling and running around. And if you get lucky and fall asleep, the nurses wake you up to take your temperature." She stopped and looked over at me, like she was waiting for me to say something dumb.

I walked over to the quilt. "This is really nice. Mrs. Benson put in a lot of work."

"It looks better from back here," Sara said. "You can't see all the misspelled words. And you can't see how lame the pictures are."

I glanced at my square. I had done a picture of a jack-o'-lantern.

"I'm not talking about yours. So don't get your little feelings hurt. I didn't say anything bad about your little pumpkin."

I wasn't going to fight with her. I kept my face turned away until I was smiling again. When I looked toward her again, she was smiling, too—that nasty little smile that said, I'm ready. Hit me with your best shot.

"Our class is going to put on a play," I said. "It'll be part of the holiday assembly."

Sara snorted. "And you'll be the star, right?"

I acted like I hadn't heard that. "We have to call it a holiday assembly. Nothing religious in it. So in chorus we're doing all these dippy songs like 'Winter Wonderland' and 'Frosty the Snowman.'"

"The only good thing about being sick," Sara said, "is missing junk like that."

I looked straight at her and forced a smile onto my face. "You'll be back to school by then. Everybody says you're doing great."

Sara gave me a rotten look. "Don't start giving me that goodie-pie stuff, you big fake. I'm sick, but I'm not dumb. And I'm not blind."

She turned away from me and looked out the window. I stood and pretended to look at the quilt. "It may start raining pretty soon," I said.

"Just what I need," Sara muttered. "The weather girl."

I kept facing the quilt. I moved my left arm in front of me so that I could see my watch. A minute went by. Then two more.

I heard a click, and the television set came on. "Time for *Mayberry R.F.D.*," Sara said. "I can't believe how old this show is. See? It's in black and white." She punched up the volume. "You can't believe the TV here. They have all the good channels blocked. Don't want anything to upset the sickies."

So I stood there and watched Andy and Opie until Mom came back. She gave Sara the Breath Savers, then said we'd better go. She didn't have to talk me into it.

"Good-bye, Sara," I said.

"Nice talking to you, Mouse Ears," Sara said, snorting to make sure I knew she didn't mean it.

I couldn't get out of that hospital fast enough. I stepped through the front door and took a deep breath. It felt good to be out in the fresh air.

I wasn't mad at Sara. She'd been in that hospital for weeks and weeks, and she'd been really sick, and all her hair had fallen out. Why shouldn't she be in a bad mood? I was mad at myself. I'd wanted to say something to make her feel better, but all I had done was stand around like a dope.

I felt sorry for her. I really did. But at the same time, I was glad it wasn't me. I know how bad that sounds. It was a rotten thing to think. But it was true.

At school the next day I had to stand up and tell about my visit. The whole class looked worried. They'd all forgotten what Sara was really like. They felt sorry for her, and they only remembered the good things about her.

"Sara's still pretty sick," I said. "She's kind of skinny, and she's lost her hair."

"She's bald-headed?" Sam asked.

"She loved the quilt," I went on. "And she

wanted me to be sure to thank everybody for it. She misses everybody and says to say hi." Vicky Waite started to sob. "And she hopes to be back in school pretty soon."

It was all a big lie, of course. And I've never been any good at lying. My mother catches me before I finish the first sentence. But that day everybody believed me. They gave me these sad smiles and shook their heads.

As soon as I sat down, four people leaned my way. They all had the same question: "She's bald-headed?"

chapter 6

MONDAY, JANUARY 25

It was late January, the first day of the new quarter and the beginning of Fresh Start, Ms. Diaz's latest idea. We were all supposed to make changes in our lives—get out of our ruts, get rid of bad habits.

On Friday we had written down things we didn't like about ourselves. Then we wrote down ways to make things better. "What if you're already perfect?" Sam asked.

When we came into the room, Ms. Diaz stood at the door and shook hands with everybody. That was her first change. And the desks had been moved so that the aisles were crooked. On the bulletin board was a big poster: TODAY IS THE FIRST DAY OF THE REST OF YOUR LIFE.

"Welcome to a new beginning," Ms. Diaz said when the last bell rang. She was wearing a bright yellow dress with a shiny black belt. "Today is even more special than I thought. I have good news for you. I'll give it to you as soon as Jacob gets here." She smiled. "Some things don't change—even with Fresh Start."

Just then Jacob threw open the door and ran into the room. Everybody broke out laughing. Jacob looked around. "What?"

When Jacob was in his seat, Ms. Diaz said, "Sara will be back this afternoon."

Everybody started talking at once. Eddie leaned forward and asked me, "You think she'll wear a wig?"

I was so surprised by the news. In early December Sara had been moved to a special children's hospital in San Francisco. We had sent letters to her every week or two, and she had sent us a couple of postcards and a thank-you note. She hadn't said a word about coming home.

"Sara has to see her doctor this morning," Ms. Diaz went on. "But she'll be here after lunch. She may only come half a day at first, anyway."

"Is she all well?" Jacob asked.

"She's doing better," Ms. Diaz said. "But she has a long way to go."

Jacob nodded. "But she's not gonna die?"

"How can you say something like that?" Vicky Waite shouted. "That's horrible. What's the matter with you?"

"What's the matter with *you*?" Jacob said. "I was just asking something."

"Sara's doing fine," Ms. Diaz said. "I was thinking about a welcome-back party. How does that sound?"

Everybody liked that idea, of course. Especially when Ms. Diaz said she'd order some cookies from the bakery. But then she said, "Shall we make a banner?"

Everybody else answered yes. But I remembered what Sara had said about the banner I'd taken her from the sixth graders: a tacky two-minute computer job. "Maybe we could do something else," I said.

Vicky was ready for war right then. "Well, I think that a banner would be great." She turned and glared at me. "Just because you don't like her—"

"That's enough," Ms. Diaz said.

People were waiting for me to say something else. But I knew better.

So Ms. Diaz appointed a banner committee (guess who wasn't selected), and they made the banner. Sara was wrong, though. It wasn't a tacky two-minute job. The committee kept getting the instructions wrong, and it took them a lot of paper and most of first period to get WELCOME BACK, SARA printed. So it was a tacky one-hour job.

Then we all signed the banner. I wanted to write, "I tried to talk them out of doing this banner." But I knew that people were going to read what I'd written. Ones like Vicky were just waiting for me to say something nasty.

So I wrote, "Here's another banner for your collection. You can put it with the one from the sixth-graders."

Mr. Craig had heard about Sara's coming back. He thought we should all write poems for her, but people kept saying they couldn't think of anything. So we ended up doing one poem from the whole class.

The poem started with "While you were gone." Then each of us had to write something to add to the poem.

Mr. Craig put the opening words on a piece of poster paper. Then, when people finished their parts, they came up and added them to the poster.

In the meantime Mr. Craig came around and talked to people about the run-a-thon. It was set for Friday, February 5. We had rain dates in case of bad weather, but in our part of California, we don't get much rain.

The run-a-thon was our school's big money-maker to buy sports equipment. That day everybody ran the track for a half hour. We were all supposed to get sponsors—people who would pay a certain amount for each lap we ran.

"Hey, Jones," Eddie whispered, "will you be a sponsor for me?"

"Come on," I said, "you're not supposed to get people from class."

"I don't know anybody else. How about a penny a lap? That won't hurt much. I'll probably only do about two laps."

"Eddie," Mr. Craig asked, "how many sponsors do you have?"

"It depends on Jones," Eddie said. "She won't give me an answer."

"The answer is no," I told him.

"I guess I don't have any sponsors," Eddie said. "And it's all Jones's fault."

Mr. Craig didn't ask me about sponsors. He knew I had a bundle. I planned to win the grand prize in the run-a-thon, a new mountain bike. I needed that bike. My old one was shot. No matter how much I oiled and fussed with it, it still squeaked and clattered. You could hear me coming a block away.

Getting sponsors had been easy. My mother is the biggest softie in the world. Whenever people have to get donations or sell cookies or magazines, they come right to my mother. She never says no. So right away I went after the parents of everybody she'd helped. Then I got all the people I knew in our neighborhood.

I was miles ahead of everybody else. But I wasn't taking any chances. I'd even been running every afternoon, getting in shape so that I could do a lot of laps in my thirty minutes.

"You guys aren't doing your part," Mr. Craig said. "It's for the good of the school. If everybody would help, this class could still win the ice-cream party."

"Man, I hate it," Sam said. "People open the door and say, 'What do you want?' Just like you're dirt. Then they slam the door before you even finish."

"Most people will be nice," Mr. Craig said. "Just be very polite."

"Oh, Mr. Craig," Sam said, "would you please, double please, sponsor me?" He laughed. "That was polite, wasn't it?"

Mr. Craig laughed. "A penny a lap. That's all I can afford."

Then everybody was yelling, "Please, Mr. Craig. What about me?"

Mr. Craig shook his head. "If you guys would work half this hard on your parents and your neighbors, you'd have no trouble at all."

I walked to the front of the room and used the marker pen to add my part to the poem:

While you were gone,
we had a play,
and everybody forgot their lines,
and Sam's Santa Claus beard fell off,
but our parents said it was great.

Eddie was waiting when I finished. "You better see this," he said.

I handed him the marker pen and watched him write:

While you were gone,
Jones signed up two million sponsors
for the run-a-thon.
The only person in town that she missed
was you. So WATCH OUT!

When the poem was finished, Mr. Craig read it aloud. "That is really great," he said. "If you guys would put in half that much effort—"

"I think I heard this before," Eddie said.

Everybody came in early after lunch period. Ms. Diaz said she'd wait for Sara in the parking lot and bring her to the room. We sat at our desks and watched the door. "Do we yell 'Surprise'?" Sam wanted to know.

Vicky thought we should all shout "Welcome back." Somebody else wanted us to yell "Hi, Sara."

Before anything was decided, Ms. Diaz pulled open the door, and Sara walked in.

Some people called out "Hi" or "Welcome back." But most people didn't get out a word. Behind me, Eddie muttered, "Oh, man."

To me, Sara didn't look so bad. She was thin, and she had bags under her eyes. But she didn't look like a ghost, the way she had in the hospital. But the other people hadn't seen her the way I had.

Sara was wearing a green warm-up suit and

an Oakland Raiders cap. She waved a hand and smiled as she looked around the room. Vicky jumped out of her seat and ran to hug Sara. Sara gave her a quick hug and stepped back. "If you start crying, Vicky, you're outa here."

"Sara," Ms. Diaz called out, "it's good to have you back." Everybody clapped.

Sara took off her cap and bowed, the way ballplayers do. A few people let out gasps when they saw her bare head.

"I thought about getting a wig," Sara said. "But they look really stupid. Besides, what's the point? My hair's growing back. I'm already a fuzzhead."

"Can I feel it?" Jacob asked her. Everything got quiet when he said that. Then somebody laughed out loud. A lot of people had probably been thinking the same thing.

"Shut up, Jacob," Vicky said. "What's the matter with you?"

Sara smiled. "We might as well get it over with." She walked over to Jacob. "Today it's

73

free. Starting tomorrow, I'm going to charge five cents a pat."

She walked up and down the aisles, letting everybody run their hands over her head. People went "Ooo" and "Wow." One boy asked, "Does it itch?"

When Sara came to Nai's desk, Nai stood up and shook her hand. "I'm glad you are back, Sara. I missed you."

That caught Sara by surprise. For just a second, I thought she was going to cry. But then she said, "Thanks, Nai. You doing okay?"

"Yes, thank you," Nai said and sat down.

When Sara moved up beside me, she muttered, "Hey, Frog Face, did you miss me, too?"

"Hi, Sara," I said. I ran my hand over her head quickly. It was kind of like petting a dog.

Sara snorted. "You didn't answer my question, you big fake."

After we had punch and cookies, Mr. Craig stopped by with the poem that we had written. He read it aloud then gave the poster to Sara.

"Thanks, everybody," she said. "This is neat." She sounded like she meant it.

Later on, Sara sat on Ms. Diaz's desk and talked about being in the hospital. Ms. Diaz asked her about things like the exercise programs and the food. Just before the bell, Brenda asked Sara, "Weren't you scared?"

Sara started to smile, but then the smile disappeared. A weird, lonesome look came into her eyes that made shivers run down my back. "I'm still scared," she said quietly. "We won't know for a long time whether the tumor will come back."

For once in my life, I was sure that Sara meant exactly what she said.

But then she shook her head and said, "It's really crazy in the hospital. One night I'm sound asleep, really sacked out, and the nurse wakes me up to give me a sleeping pill."

Everybody else laughed, but I kept thinking about that look in Sara's eyes.

When the bell rang, Ms. Diaz folded up the

WELCOME BACK banner and gave it to Sara. I watched Sara carefully, but she smiled the whole time.

I waited until most of the others were gone, then walked past Sara. "I'm glad you're doing better," I said.

"What's the matter, Jenny?" Sara said. "Nobody to fight with? Must have been pretty boring."

"Yeah," I said.

"Hey, Sweat Sock," she muttered. "You want a tacky banner? I'll let you have it cheap."

chapter **7**

TUESDAY, JANUARY 26

Next day the school bus was noisier than usual. Three sixth-grade girls were singing, and all the boys were making fun of them.

In front of me a first-grade boy was crying because he'd left his lunch box home. "No problem," I told him. "Just go to the office. The secretary will give you a slip so that you can eat in the cafeteria."

The boy gave me a scared look. "Go to the office? I'd rather not eat."

I started thinking about Sara and that weird look I'd seen in her eyes. She was afraid, and I didn't blame her. How could she *not* be afraid?

I felt sorry for her. She was putting on a good act, but it was still an act. Maybe she seemed like the same old Sara to other people. But she didn't fool me. She was scared to death.

It was funny to think about. Sara and I were *not* friends. Or we were worst friends anyway. But in a way I knew her better than anybody else.

I wanted to help her. I couldn't make her get well, but maybe I could be her friend. And right then Sara needed all the friends she could get. Especially somebody she couldn't fool.

I knew it wouldn't be easy. I had been fighting with Sara for years, and that's what she'd expect. But I could do it. I just had to think before I opened my big mouth.

I remembered Ms. Diaz's Fresh Start. The

first step, she said, was writing down your goal. Putting it on paper made it real.

I turned to a fresh page in my notebook and wrote in big block letters, SARA NEEDS A REAL FRIEND AND I WILL BE THAT FRIEND. I underlined each word three times.

I tried to think about being Sara's friend, but it wasn't easy. When Brenda slept over at my house, we stayed up late and ate microwave popcorn and watched monster movies. It was hard to picture doing that with Sara.

For now, I just wouldn't fight with her. That was a good beginning—a fresh start. Then we'd see.

When I got off the bus, I saw Brenda playing two-square with some third-graders. "Come on and play," she called to me.

I looked around the playground. "Is Sara here?"

"She's over on the bench," Brenda said. "Rotten brat. I don't care if she is sick. She's still a big brat."

"What's the matter?" I asked.

"I was trying to be nice to her," Brenda said. "I told her I was sorry about her hair. And you know what she said? She said, 'You're the one I feel sorry for. I have ugly hair and you have an ugly face. My hair will grow out, and you'll still have an ugly face.' "

"She was making a joke," I said.

"She was being a brat," Brenda said. "She's always been a brat."

I walked across to the bench where Sara was sitting. All kinds of people were standing around her. "Hey, Bean Brain," she called to me, "I have something for you." She held out a can, about the size of a soup can. People started laughing, so I knew something was wrong.

The label on the can was made out of note-book paper. Printed on it was RATTLESNAKE IN A CAN. Below that was a picture of a snake and red writing that said DANGER and OPEN WITH CARE.

"Go ahead," Sara said. "Open it up."

"No thanks," I said.

Sara laughed. "You're not afraid, are you? You don't really believe there's a snake in there?"

I knew it was some kind of joke. Probably a jack-in-the-box—a big snake that would pop out. So I pointed the can away from me and took off the lid.

Bzzzzzzzzzzzzz!

When I heard the rattling sound, I dropped the can and jumped back. And, of course, everybody laughed like crazy.

"Nai brought it to me," Sara said. "We were just waiting for a dummy to come along so we could test it. And here came Jenny."

Everybody laughed like that was the funniest joke they'd ever heard. I felt my cheeks get warm, but I caught myself and smiled. It was my first chance *not* to fight back. And I made it.

I picked up the can. "This is neat." Inside the can was a little stick with a rubber band wrapped around it.

"I saw one in the store," Nai said. "It cost too much, so I made one at home."

"Can I borrow it?" Eddie asked. "I want to try it on my sister."

"Sure," Sara said. "Go find another dummy."

Eddie and Nai went off toward the tetherball poles.

Some first-graders came up and whispered something to Sara. She laughed and said, "I ought to make you pay for this." She knelt down while they touched her hair. It was funny to watch them. Some of them giggled. Some were scared. They acted like the hair might burn them.

"So, Jenny," Sara said, "I hear you've been the big deal while I was gone. Star of the Christmas play. First prize in the run-a-thon."

"I wasn't the star," I said. "Sam was. He played Santa Claus."

"And his beard fell off," Vicky said. "It was so funny."

"And we haven't had the run-a-thon yet," I said.

Sara gave me one of her sneaky smiles—the kind she gets when she's just put gum on your seat. I wondered what rotten thing she was thinking about.

But I smiled and said, "I'm glad you're back, Sara."

That caught her by surprise. She just stared at me.

When we went into the room, Sam whispered to me, "Look what I got." He lifted the lid of his desk and showed me a camera.

"What's the big deal?" I asked.

"I'm going to take Sara's picture," Sam said. "Right now she's being pretty nice to me. But it won't last. By the time her hair grows out, she'll be the same old Sara. So I want to have this picture ready. When she starts laughing at me about my math scores, I'll show her the picture."

"Leave her alone," I said.

Sam gave me a funny look. "What's your trouble?"

"Just leave her alone. I'm serious."

Sam shook his head and sat down. "You must be having a bad, bad day."

Ms. Diaz raised her hand for people to be quiet. She was wearing a white dress with big sunflowers on it. "I have something to read," she announced. She read a note from our principal, Mrs. Baker, giving the rules about smoking.

"We've only heard this about fifty times," Sam muttered.

"I can't believe anybody is that stupid," Ms. Diaz said. "But I guess someone has been smoking in the rest room."

Behind me, Eddie started to giggle.

"What's so funny?" I asked him.

"Nobody's smoking," Eddie whispered. "You know Billy Kramer, that sixth-grader? He's mad at Mrs. Baker because he brought a frog to school and she took it away from him.

He knows how bad Mrs. Baker hates smoking. So he picks up cigarette butts off the street and leaves them in the bathroom."

"That's pretty dumb," I said.

"So's Billy Kramer," Eddie said.

While we were doing math, Ms. Diaz worked with Sara. Then Ms. Diaz came to my desk and asked if I'd help Sara. "Sure," I said. "If it's okay with her."

Ms. Diaz smiled. "It was her idea."

Sara and I went to the back of the room. "I missed a lot," Sara said. "Vicky was trying to help me, but in math she's dumber than dirt."

For most of an hour we worked together. Sara caught on fast, and we went through fifteen pages. She hated being behind, so she didn't talk about anything but math. Until the bell rang. Then she said, "Okay, Turtle Nose, now you can go brag to everybody about how much you helped me."

"You're welcome," I said before I thought.

Sara almost smiled. I figured that for once we just might get along.

I should have known better.

The first thing Mr. Craig said to us that day was, "I'm ashamed of you people." Then he looked at me and said, "I'm not talking to you, Jennifer. I'm talking to the rest of these people."

Mr. Craig was talking about the run-a-thon, of course. Even with all the pledges I had turned in, our class was behind all the other classes.

"You're not doing this for me," Mr. Craig said. "You're doing this for yourselves. The money helps all of you."

Right then Sara raised her hand. "Mr. Craig," she said, "is it too late to enter the run-a-thon?"

Mr. Craig smiled. "Of course not."

"I can't go very fast right now," Sara said. "But I think I can make it around the track once in half an hour. If I stop and rest a few times."

"Do you guys hear that?" Mr. Craig said. "Sara's been really sick, and she's willing to do her part. Doesn't that make you feel bad?" He walked over to Sara's desk. "I'll tell you what, Sara. If you can't make it around, I'll carry you." Then he laughed. "I have a better idea. You'll make more than one lap. I'll push you around in a wheelbarrow. How's that?"

Everybody laughed at first. Then Eddie called out, "I'll sponsor you for that, Sara."

"Me, too," yelled Sam.

Mr. Craig got a sponsor sheet for Sara, and in five minutes half the class had signed it. Sara kept looking over at me with a nasty smile on her face. I wasn't worried then. It would take more than Eddie's pennies for her to catch me.

During lunch, Vicky and some of the other girls went around the playground getting people to sign Sara's sheet. "What about you, Mouse Ears?" Sara said. "Are you going to be my sponsor? Or are you afraid I'm gonna win your prize?"

She was waiting for me to say no, but I said, "Sure, Sara." I signed for five cents a lap. I didn't think it would cost me more than a quarter. I couldn't see Mr. Craig doing more than five laps with a wheelbarrow.

"You're crazy," Sara said. "Why would you help me?"

"Why not?" I said. "The school needs the money."

Sara just shook her head.

That afternoon Mr. Craig came to our classroom and said, "I need to borrow Sara for a little while."

Ms. Diaz smiled. "Just don't keep her too long."

"Let's go, Sara," Mr. Craig said. "You're going to be on television."

That got everybody going, of course.

"The people from Channel Eleven are here," Mr. Craig said.

Sara ran her hand over her head. "Oh, gee, I'd better comb my hair."

Sara went off with Mr. Craig, and everybody begged Ms. Diaz to let us go watch. "You people have work to do," she said.

So we stayed in the room, but nobody did any work.

When Sara came back, Ms. Diaz let her tell us about it. "There was just one woman. Paula Pine. The dark-haired one on the news. She set up the camera and then came and talked to Mr. Craig and me."

"Sara's gonna be a star," Eddie called out.

"That's right," Sara said. "Six o'clock news on Channel Eleven." Then she looked straight at me and gave me that same sneaky smile. I knew right then that I was finished.

I watched the news that night. Paula Pine got tears in her eyes when she talked about the brave girl who wanted to help her school. And with her bald head and white face, Sara looked

91

like she might fall down and die any minute. "I just want to do my part," she said, looking straight into the camera. "I'm going to get well, and pretty soon I'll be using the sports equipment just like everybody else."

Then they showed Mr. Craig pushing Sara in the wheelbarrow while Paula gave people a telephone number where they could call and make their pledges.

When the program went back to the studio, the news people all said they were going to pledge. The phone number kept showing on the screen.

A few minutes later our telephone rang. When I answered it, Sara said, "Hey, Bug Breath, have you called in your pledge yet?"

I kept my voice quiet. "I signed up at school, remember?"

"That was something," Sara said. "Didn't it make your old heart go pitty-pat?" She let out a nasty laugh. "You know what's really funny? I'll probably win that stupid bicycle, and I already have one that's better than that. And I'm not supposed to ride a bike anyway."

"I have to go," I said and hung up the phone. Then I went over to my notebook and looked at the note I had written: SARA NEEDS A REAL FRIEND AND I WILL BE THAT FRIEND. I tore out the page and ripped it into little tiny pieces.

But after I had done that, I felt worse.

chapter 8

FRIDAY, FEBRUARY 5

It was run-a-thon day. Finally. I was sick of the whole thing. Sara had been on the news almost every night for the past two weeks. She had over $500 in pledges for each lap she made. If Mr. Craig got her around the track once, she'd be the winner. And Mr. Craig would do more than one lap. He'd been working out after school with a loaded wheel-barrow.

"I don't have a chance," I told Eddie that morning. "I could run ten miles, and I wouldn't even be close to Sara."

"Yeah, Jones," Eddie said, running his hand through his hair. "But I wouldn't want to trade places with her."

And he was right, of course. I was feeling sorry for myself about a bicycle, and Sara might die.

That's the way things had been for two weeks. Every time I started to get mad at Sara, I felt like a rotten brat.

But there was a part of me that still got mad. Sara was different now. She was being pretty nice to everybody but Brenda and me. And the only reason Brenda was treated rotten was because she was my friend.

Sara called me names and made fun of my clothes the way she always did. But now, instead of fighting back, I just smiled.

So Sara found new ways to get to me. I hated it when Sara made fun of the people who were helping her. And she knew it. So she piled it on.

95

"Vicky's loving every minute of this," Sara would whisper to me. "If I die, she'll probably wear black for years." And I smiled.

When two girls brought her flowers one day, she was nice as she could be. Then she came over to my desk and whispered, "They brought me flowers. Isn't that sweet? And they're so proud of themselves. It's enough to make me puke." And I smiled.

After the news one night, she phoned me and said, "Did you see what Mr. Craig was doing? He was shoving me out of the way so he could get his pretty face on the camera. This is his big chance to be famous." And that time I didn't have to smile because we were on the phone.

But even while she was being terrible, I could tell that she was scared. She looked about the same and sounded about the same, but something wasn't quite right. And I was the only one who knew.

So I kept being nice. But it wasn't easy. I felt

sorry for her, but sometimes I also felt like dumping a bucket of ice water on her nasty bald head. And that made me feel like a spoiled brat, too.

I didn't say anything, though. I stayed nice. Sometimes I ended up biting my tongue. And I kept forcing dumb smiles on my face when I wanted to scream.

But I stayed nice. I was the only one who knew how mad I got sometimes, how much I was holding back. Or maybe I wasn't the only one. Now and then I'd catch Sara watching me with a funny look on her face, and I got the feeling that she could read my mind.

Our class was scheduled to run at ten-thirty, so we were supposed to have regular class until then. But people were too excited to settle down to their math books. And why not? With all of Sara's pledges, our class was bound to win the ice-cream party. And the TV crew was going to be there.

Since we were all talking about the run-a-thon, Ms. Diaz decided that we should do a different kind of math. She had everybody figure out how much money they would bring in if they ran four laps. Or three. Or nine.

"This isn't fair," Sara said, laughing. "Mine is harder than everybody else's."

Boo hoo, I thought. But I kept smiling.

"Mine's not too tough," Eddie whispered. "I have pledges for nine cents a lap."

The class ended up working with Sara's pledges. We started out with regular numbers, but then Ms. Diaz decided that we should think big. We figured out that Sara could earn a million dollars if Mr. Craig could do 1,912 laps. The only problem was that he'd have to do about 64 laps a minute, which was 960 miles an hour.

By ten o'clock we were tired of math problems, and Ms. Diaz said that we could go out and warm up, as long as we stayed out of the way. So we ended up watching the sixth-graders run. Which was about as exciting as doing math problems.

To make people run harder, Mr. Craig had announced extra prizes—Burger King gift certificates for the boy and girl in each grade who ran the most laps. That didn't help much in the sixth grade. Nai's big brother, Kao, was two laps ahead of everybody else after the first ten minutes. And only one girl was running hard.

But things changed when the Channel 11 van pulled in. When Paula Pine climbed out of the van with her camera, you should have seen people start running.

Sara was wearing a blue warm-up suit. "Blue's a good color for TV," she whispered to me.

After the sixth-graders were finished, Paula got all of us lined up on the track. "We want to get the beginning of the race," she said. "I want you all to bunch up together, shoulder to shoulder. The camera doesn't like spaces in between. And we'll get Sara sitting in the wheelbarrow right in the middle."

She lined us all up, putting shorter ones close to the wheelbarrow, then tall ones behind and on the sides. She had the camera on a tripod and kept checking through the viewfinder. "That's looking really good," she called out. "Now, just before you start, I want some of you to go over, one at a time, and shake hands with Sara. Smile and say, 'Good luck' or something like that. The rest of you keep smiling."

Right away I was picked to shake hands. I showed my teeth to the camera and went over to Sara. With a big smile on her face, she whispered, "Too bad we're gonna kick your fanny, Giraffe Legs."

I kept the corners of my mouth pulled back. "Good luck, Sara."

"I won't need it," she said, still smiling.

When I saw that scene on the six o'clock news, we looked so happy and sweet, it was enough to make me sick.

All the other classes started their run by having somebody yell, "Go!" But Paula Pine had brought a starter's pistol for Mrs. Baker to use. Mrs. Baker said she didn't know much about guns, but all she had to do was point it up in the air and pull the trigger. She let out a big "Oh!" when the pistol fired.

The TV camera was set up on the track, and we were all supposed to run straight until we were past the camera. But half the people ran right for the camera so they could be sure to be on TV.

On the first lap, most people tried to stay next to Sara and the wheelbarrow because that's where the TV camera was pointing. So none of them were moving very fast. Mr. Craig was doing his best, but you don't break speed records pushing a wheelbarrow.

I left the wheelbarrow behind right away. It felt good to be moving. I kept a steady pace and shook my hands to relax. Nai ran along beside me. "Can you run this way for thirty minutes?" he asked.

"We'll see," I said.

Nai laughed, as if I had made a joke. "May I run with you for a while?"

"Sure," I said. "Just so I don't hold you back."

Nai laughed again. "I will have a hard time keeping up with you."

Nai stayed right at my shoulder. Pretty soon I was puffing like a train, but he was still talking easily, not even out of breath. "I think we will win the ice-cream party," he said. "What ice cream do you like best?"

"Chocolate," I said. Actually, my favorite is Jamocha Almond Fudge, but I didn't have enough breath to say that. When we passed the wheelbarrow a second time, we had to swing wide to go around all the people. Sara waved to us when we went by. "You look tired, Jenny," she called.

After the first lap or two, I kept my eyes on the track in front of me, so I missed some of the action. Mrs. Baker caught Sam and Eddie taking a shortcut across the track, and two or three people sneaked off and hid in the rest rooms until the time was up. Once, about twenty minutes along, Sara got out of the wheelbarrow and walked alongside to give Mr. Craig a little rest. She did that right in front of the TV camera, of course.

Nai kept running beside me. When I was puffing too hard to talk, he ended up telling me stories about his father learning to drive a car. And about his little sister getting lost in the Kmart store.

When the thirty minutes were finally up, Nai and I had run fourteen laps. Three and a half miles. "Thank you, Nai," I said. "I've never run that far before."

Nai smiled. "I never talked that much before."

Mr. Craig had made five laps, so the school had plenty of money for the sports program. He lay down on the grass and didn't move. Sara stood over him, smiling while the TV camera rolled.

We ended up back in class with about a half hour until lunch. Mr. Craig said, "Free reading today. It's okay to talk, but keep the noise down." He sank into a chair and closed his eyes.

People were excited about the ice-cream party, and they did a lot more talking than reading. I didn't do either one. I put my head on my desk and almost went to sleep.

Just before lunch Sara came and knelt down beside my desk. "Poor little Jenny, is she tired?"

"What do you think?" I said.

"I think I'm going to win a bicycle," Sara said. "And I don't even want it." She tapped me on the arm. "If I was a nice person, I'd give it to my good pal, Jennifer Rae Jones—better known as Jenny Bray."

"Oh, sure."

"I mean, you really deserve it. You collected all those pledges and ran so hard."

I closed my eyes again.

"Hey, Sara," Eddie said, "if Jones doesn't want it, I'll take it."

Sara laughed. "Oh, she wants it, all right. But her mommy taught her not to beg." She tapped me on the arm again. "Wake up, Sleeping Sweaty—I mean, Sleeping Beauty. If I was nice and gave you the bike, you'd take it, wouldn't you?"

I raised my head, but I didn't answer her.

"But Jenny already has some prizes," Sara said. "Maybe a bike would be too much. We don't want to spoil her."

I put my head back on my desk, facing the other way.

After Sara went back to her seat, Eddie asked me, "You think she'll give you the bike?"

"No." Right then I thought it was just barely possible. It was the kind of surprise that Sara might go for. But I wasn't going to say so.

At two o'clock we had the awards assembly. We all crowded into the multipurpose room and sat on the cold floor. Mr. Craig was trying to get the speaker system to work. Every time he spoke into the microphone, the speakers squawked. Finally he brought out an old speaker system that made him sound like Bugs Bunny. He waved his fist and yelled, "I'm proud of you."

Mrs. Baker gave a speech, and so did the head of the Parents' Club. They both sounded like Bugs Bunny. I didn't hear most of what they said. I was watching Sara, who kept looking over at me and smiling.

After the speeches, Mr. Craig gave out the Burger King certificates to the people who had run the most laps. He had all of the winners come get their prizes then stay up in front. He called my name for the winning girl in our class. Then he announced that I had run more laps than any other girl in the school. So I got two prizes.

Then Mr. Craig announced the prizes for raising money, starting with a bunch of people who got school T-shirts. While the T-shirts were being handed out, Paula Pine came in the door with her TV camera. She came right down in front and stood in the middle of the third-graders. She set up her camera, and some of the people onstage started to smile. But I could see that the red recording light wasn't on.

The next prizes were sweatshirts and movie tickets. I already knew what I'd get—a backpack for second place. When I stepped up to get my prize, Mr. Craig shook my hand while he talked about how hard I had worked and how fast I had run. I glanced down at Paula and saw that the television camera still wasn't running.

Then Mrs. Baker brought out the bicycle, and Mr. Craig announced that Sara was the winner. Sara stood up like this was a big surprise, and she took her time walking to the front. Mrs. Baker gave a long speech about Sara and the wonderful people in our town. She said that Sara had raised almost three thousand dollars.

While everybody was cheering for Sara, she

turned back and smiled at me. Then she took the microphone and said, "Thank you. But I don't deserve this prize. All I did was sit in the wheelbarrow while Mr. Craig pushed it. And everybody in town gave money. Besides, I can't even ride a bicycle right now. These days the only way I travel is the Internet—when I can get my mom off the computer. So what I want to do is this."

She stopped for a second and turned back just far enough so that she could see me out of the corner of her eye. Right then I could feel a lump in my throat. She was actually going to do it. Sara, my old worst friend, was going to give me the bike.

"I want this bike to go to somebody who can use it," Sara said. "So I'm giving it to the Girls Club. They need bikes for their after-school program."

Everybody clapped while a woman from the Girls Club came up and took the bike. I think I clapped, but I don't remember.

Since the woman was already there, I knew

that Sara had planned all this ahead of time. So she had made a real sucker out of me.

But I wasn't going to let her know. When she walked back to stand by me, I used my nicest voice to say, "That was a really sweet thing to do, Sara."

Sara put her arm around me and waved. "Smile, Frog Face," she whispered. "You're going to be on TV tonight."

chapter 9

MONDAY, FEBRUARY 8

I was still mad on Monday. Not because I didn't get the bicycle that I'd worked so hard for. I could live without the bike. What still had me grinding my teeth was Sara's little act.

That was pure nastiness. A rotten trick to get my hopes up so that she could stomp them into the ground.

On the playground before school, I stayed

away from Sara. I was still going to be nice to her, but it would be easier if I didn't see her right then.

When I came into the classroom, Sara was sitting on her desk with a bunch of girls around her. "Here's Jenny," Sara called out. "The fastest girl in the school. Where's your brand-new second-prize backpack?"

I squeezed a smile onto my face. "I didn't have a chance to clean out my old one yet."

"I thought maybe you were pouting," Sara said. "I thought maybe you weren't happy with your prize."

"No, it's fine." I went straight to my desk.

Eddie was leaning back in his chair. "Hey, Jones, you gonna give me your old backpack?"

"What would you do with a backpack?" I said. "You haven't taken a book home all year."

"That's not true, Jones," Eddie said. "I took my English book home last month. Don't you remember? Mr. Craig got mad at me because I kept forgetting to bring it back."

Ms. Diaz came down the aisle. She was wearing her butterfly dress—a green dress with pictures of butterflies all over it. "Good job on Friday, Jennifer," she said. "Fourteen laps. That's amazing. It would take me about a week to do fourteen laps."

I smiled and said thank you.

"Oh, thank you," Sara said in this fake voice that didn't sound a bit like me. But all the girls around her laughed just the same.

"We get our party tomorrow afternoon," Ms. Diaz called out. "If you're absent, you're out of luck."

"Does everybody get to go to the party?" Vicky asked. "Even those people who sneaked off and hid in the rest room?"

Ms. Diaz looked surprised. "I'm sure nobody in here would do a childish thing like that." While she said that, she looked straight at the ones who had done it.

Two minutes after the final bell rang, Jacob Smalley came rushing into the room. "It's not my fault," he yelled out.

Ms. Diaz smiled. "It never is. Why should today be any different?"

"I would have been here on time, but the Channel Eleven van was out in front. Paula Pine was taking pictures of the building, and she needed somebody handsome to be in the picture."

"What's she doing back here?" Sam asked.

"We're going to have an assembly right away," Jacob said.

"That's news to me," Ms. Diaz said.

Right then a sixth-grader came in with a note, asking us to come for a short assembly. "Don't mess with me," Jacob said. "I know what's happening."

We filed out the door and went to the multipurpose room. We sat down on the cold floor and watched Mrs. Baker fumbling with the microphone. She was using the old speaker system again, and she still sounded like Bugs Bunny. Paula Pine stood in the back with her camera on her shoulder.

Mrs. Baker had Nai's brother, Kao, lead the Pledge of Allegiance because Kao had run the farthest on Friday. Then she announced how much money had been raised by the school. She talked about the great help we had gotten from the people in town.

"One of those people is here with us," she went on. "This is Mr. Taylor from the Computer Corral."

Mr. Taylor was wearing a cowboy hat and a string tie. He grabbed the mike and held it up close to his mouth as if he were going to sing. "It's an honor to be here," he said, sounding even more like Bugs Bunny than Mrs. Baker did.

Mr. Taylor talked for a long time about responsibility and hard work. It was hard to understand him, and I kept wondering why he was there. While he was talking, Paula Pine came over with her camera and stood just to one side of Sara.

Finally Mr. Taylor said he'd been watching the news last Friday night. "When I saw the young lady give away her bicycle, that really touched me. That same young lady said that she did her traveling on the Internet, so we at Computer Corral wanted to make it easier for her. We're giving her a computer of her very own."

The TV camera was on Sara's face, of course. She gave them a show. Her mouth dropped open first. Then she smiled and let out a yell. When I saw her that night on the six o'clock news, she reminded me of the contestants on *The Price Is Right*.

Sara came up to the front, with Paula Pine following her. Mr. Taylor brought out a table with the computer on it. He put his arm around Sara and smiled for the TV.

After a minute, Sara took the mike and said, "Thank you. Thank you, everybody.

I'm the luckiest person in this school." That got the whole place cheering, and it choked up the whole broadcast bunch that night on the news.

When we came back to our classroom, Ms. Diaz did some math drills to get us thinking about math again. Then she put some problems on the board for us to work.

Before I could get out my paper, Ms. Diaz came to my desk and asked if I would help Sara today. "We're going to spend the hour reviewing for Wednesday's test," she said. "You don't need the review."

Sara asked if we could study outside where it was quiet, and Ms. Diaz let us go. As soon as we were out the door, Sara said, "I'm glad to get out of that room. I don't feel like doing math this morning."

"But that's why we're out here," I said, sitting down on a bench.

Sara waved me away. "Oh, listen to you. You sound like Mrs. Baker. You want to give me a little talk about responsibility like old Tex from the Computer Corral?"

"If you don't want to work, that's okay with me," I said. "You're the one who's behind."

"So what? You think I'll get a bad grade? You're out of your mind. All the teachers feel sorry for me. I'll bet I get straight A's this quarter. It doesn't matter what I get on the tests."

I just smiled. Or tried to.

"Don't look up," Sara said, sitting down beside me and opening her book. "Mrs. Baker is watching us from her window. You'd think she had better things to do."

I opened my book. "Where did we quit last time?"

Sara shut her book. "She's gone now. Let's go over to the rest room where nobody can spy on us."

"Nobody's spying on us now," I said.

"Oh, come on, Jenny," Sara said. "You won't get in trouble. A poor sick kid like me—I can go to the bathroom anytime I want."

We walked across the playground to the rest room. Sara went to a sink and got her hand wet, then rubbed it on her head. "I think I sunburned my scalp last Friday."

"You got a computer out of the deal," I said. "That oughta be worth a sunburn."

"Big whoop," Sara said. "Probably some old floor model that Tex wanted to get rid of. It's not even a Mac. That's what I'm used to."

"Oh, boo-hoo," I said before I caught myself.

"Maybe I should go on TV again," Sara said. "Maybe I could give this one away and get some other sucker to give me a Mac. I could give them a little tear maybe. They'd eat that up."

I couldn't stand it any longer. "Why do you act this way?" I screamed. "Everybody's nice to you, and you're rotten. What's the matter with you?"

"Just a brain tumor," Sara said, and she gave me this nasty smile.

"I know you had a brain tumor," I yelled. "But what do you want? Everybody's nice to you."

"Even Jenny, who can't stand me. So sweet, sugar wouldn't melt in her mouth."

"I've been nice to you," I shouted. "So what? So has everybody else."

"And I know why you're being nice. You think I'm gonna die, don't you?"

"That's so dumb," I yelled.

"I don't think so," Sara said, keeping her voice quiet so that I'd sound even stupider. "If you don't think I'm gonna die, why are you being such a little goody-goody? You make me sick acting that way."

"I've been nice to you," I yelled. "Is that so terrible?"

"I don't want you to be nice," Sara said. "I had a brain tumor. Big deal. I don't need any special treatment. I just want to be treated like everybody else."

"Don't make me laugh," I shouted. "If you

were anybody else, you'd get your spoiled rotten rear end kicked around the block."

Sara gave me this nasty smile. "And who'd do the kicking? You? Fat chance." She reached out and gave me a little shove.

I slapped her hand away and pushed her back, hard. "Don't touch me."

Sara kept that smile on her face. "I'll touch you if I want to. I'm the girl with the brain tumor, remember? You have to be nice to me." She stepped toward me, holding her hands out in front of her.

"Don't even think about it!" I yelled.

Sara smiled and shoved at me with both hands. I tried to grab her hands, but I only caught one. The other banged into my shoulder and knocked me back.

I yanked on the hand I had grabbed, and Sara tripped and fell against me. We both ended up on the floor. She landed on top of me, but I threw my leg over her and rolled onto her while she pounded my shoulders and back.

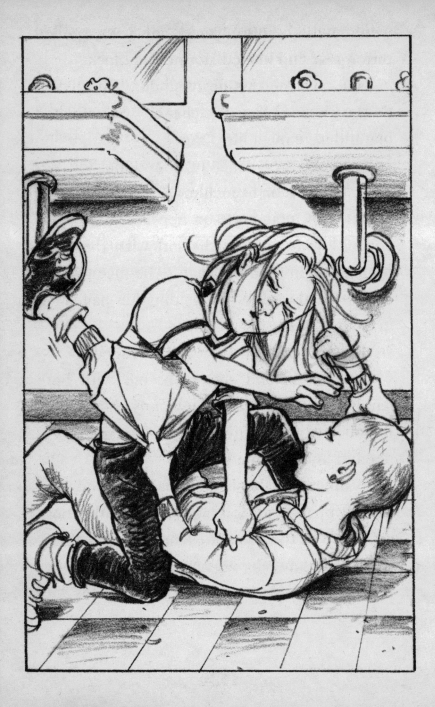

She started squirming and kicking, and we rolled over and over.

I ended up on top again. I tried to pin her arms down, but she reached up and grabbed a handful of my hair and gave it a yank. "Ouch!" I yelled. Without thinking, I reached for hers and ended up with my hand on her slick head. "That's not fair," I said.

And all of a sudden we were laughing. We lay there on the tile floor of the rest room and laughed and laughed.

"I hate to think what we've been rolling around in," Sara said, wiping tears from her eyes.

"This is so dumb," I said. "I've never been in a fight in my whole life."

"That doesn't surprise me," Sara said. "You're rotten at it."

"Hey, I was beating you," I said.

"You're dreaming, Marshmallow. I'm a poor sick weakling, and I was whipping you."

"Something's wrong with your memory," I

said. "Maybe you hit your head when I threw you on the ground."

Sara laughed. "You threw me? I knocked *you* down."

I laughed, too. "I hate to tell you this, but you're a crummy fighter. And, besides, you cheat."

"Me?" Sara said. "You did everything but bite."

I looked over at her. "Are we going to fight any more?"

"I hope not," Sara said, smiling. "I hope you learned your lesson."

Just then Mrs. Baker came through the door. She stood with her mouth open and looked down at Sara and me, sitting in the middle of the floor. Finally she said, "Are you all right?"

"I just got a little dizzy," Sara said. "So I sat down for a minute."

"Do you want me to call your mother?"

"I'm feeling better now," Sara said. "I think everything's going to be fine."

Mrs. Baker stood by the door and watched us while we got up and washed our hands and faces. I tried not to look at Sara. I was afraid that if I did, I'd break out laughing.

"Hey, Jenny," Sara whispered. "You've got toilet paper stuck to the back of your head."

That was too much for me. I started to laugh. That got Sara going, and we ended up giggling like first-graders. Mrs. Baker was still standing there, so Sara and I tried to stop laughing. But as soon as we looked at each other, we'd start again.

"All right, girls," Mrs. Baker said finally. "Go on back to class. And let's try to act a little more grown-up."

Sara turned to me and said, "Yeah, Jenny." Then she crossed her eyes and stuck out her tongue. And we both broke out laughing again.

Mrs. Baker just shook her head.

chapter 10

TUESDAY, FEBRUARY 9

Our party started right after lunch. Ms. Diaz brought in a big-screen TV and a VCR. While we ate our ice cream, we watched the clips from the TV news. Ms. Diaz kept rewinding the tape so that we could see ourselves again and again.

Then Ms. Diaz started awarding prizes (lollipops and gum). Nai and I got prizes for running fourteen laps. Brenda got a prize for the most blisters. Eddie got a prize for the biggest smile on TV. Vicky got a prize for her orange shoelaces. By the time Ms. Diaz was finished, everybody had a prize.

"Now," Ms. Diaz said, "I have a few special awards to make." On the board she wrote the word EZIRP. "See that? That's *prize* spelled backward. E-zurp. Got it?"

Most people nodded, but a few people shook their heads.

"It's like a booby prize," Ms. Diaz said. "I have an ezirp for Sara for attendance." She handed Sara a lollipop.

"I only missed three or four months," Sara said.

"And I have an ezirp for Jacob for being on time," Ms. Diaz said.

"That's mean," Jacob said, laughing.

"And an ezirp for Robby Dodge for his musical contributions."

Robby stood up, took a bow, and burped out

half of "Happy Birthday to You" before Ms. Diaz cut him off.

"And I have ezirps for good sportsmanship for the people who sneaked away from the track and didn't put in their thirty minutes." She held out lollipops, but nobody went to collect them.

"And I have a special ezirp for Sam for neatness." Sam laughed and raised the lid of his desk. The desk was stuffed full of old paper bags and sandwich wrappers.

"We should have a big ezirp for Jenny Jones," Sara said. "For being so nice and sweet."

"And one for you, too," I said. "For your personality and your terrific hairdo."

Sara got a hurt look on her face and sobbed, "You're so mean." She put her head down on her desk.

The whole class was dead silent for about half a minute. Everybody stared at me. I felt my face getting hot. Then some whispering started. Finally Vicky stood up and shouted at

me, "You're so terrible. How can you be so hateful?"

Other people muttered, "Yeah."

I sat there, too surprised to say anything.

Just then, Sara sat up, laughing out loud. "Oh, give us a break, Vicky," she said. "I'm just playing."

Things got quiet again. People were feeling a little silly about getting tricked.

"Sara—" Ms. Diaz started.

Sara stood up and looked around the room. "Listen, all of you. If Jenny and I are fighting, I don't need anybody to take care of me. Okay?" She looked around at people, and they nodded.

Sara looked over at me and smiled. "And Jenny doesn't need anybody to take care of her either. Right, Jenny Bray?"

"That's right, Sara Louise," I said.

"So," Sara said, "let's all try to act a little more grown-up."

And just as if we'd practiced it, Sara and I crossed our eyes and stuck out our tongues.

chapter 11

MONDAY, JUNE 21

School has only been out for a couple of weeks, but I kind of miss it. Swimming lessons start next week, and I'm playing softball on Tuesday and Thursday, but things are still pretty quiet.

Sara and her mother came by the other day. Sara brought her laptop computer, and we played Battleship. I beat her three games to two.

"I let you win, so you wouldn't cry," she said.

Sara's hair is growing out. It's still short, but it doesn't look bad. She said that a stranger had asked who did her hair.

She feels great, but she says you have to go five years before the doctors are sure you're cured. "It's not that big a deal," she told me. "And there are no guarantees, anyway. While I'm waiting to see if I'm well, I could get hit by a bus."

She's really good with her computer. She has E-mail buddies all over the world, including a ten-year-old in Pakistan who asked her to marry him.

I get E-mail from her, too. The latest one came this morning:

NEW DIET PLAN. GUARANTEED TO WORK!
WANT TO GET RID OF 20 POUNDS OF UGLY FAT?
CUT OFF YOUR HEAD. (:

Do you think I answered something like that? Do you really think I sent a nasty note back to poor little Sara, the girl with the brain tumor?

You bet I did.